Listen up!
Grandpa Turkey, the fastest-talking
story-teller down on the farm, is
about to tell one of his famous
TALL TALES...

*For Sam Phillips, Bill Black, Scotty Moore
and Jamie Van Eaton*

ORCHARD BOOKS
96 Leonard Street, London EC2A 4XD
Orchard Books Australia
Unit 31/56 O'Riordan Street, Alexandria, NSW 2015
First published in Great Britain in 2001
First paperback edition 2002
Copyright © Jonathan Allen 2001
The right of Jonathan Allen to be identified as the author
and illustrator of this work has been asserted by him in
accordance with the Copyright, Designs, and Patents Act, 1988.
A CIP catalogue record for this book is available
from the British Library.
ISBN 1 84121 875 8 (hardback)
ISBN 1 84121 877 4 (paperback)
1 3 5 7 9 10 8 6 4 2 (hardback)
1 3 5 7 9 10 8 6 4 2 (paperback)
Printed in Great Britain

THE KING OF THE BIRDS

Jonathan Allen

ORCHARD BOOKS

"Grandpa Turkey?" said Tiny Turk one day. "Who's the king of the birds?"

Grandpa Turkey chuckled. "King of the birds? Why, the great big eagle is king of the birds!" he said.

Then he winked.

"But there was a time, Tiny Turk, when they called me the King of the Birds! It's true, listen…"

It all started when I was about the same age as you are now. I was scrabbling and scraping behind the old barn, when I came across a funny-looking thing which made a sound when I pecked at it.

I didn't know it then, but that thing was going to change my life!

"Do you know what that is?" said my friend, Sid Rooster. "That's a guitar. You can play music on it."

"I can?" I said, and picked it up.

I ran my feathers over the strings
and it made a wonderful noise.

I was hooked.

PLING!
PLONG!

Every day I
messed around
with that guitar.

CHUNGA!
CHUNGA!

And every day my playing
got better and better.

I even wrote a song.
It went something like this:

I got a crest on my head,
handsome feathers on my back.
When I play my music
all the chicks say, "Look at that!
Man, it's Turkey Boy!
Yes it is, it's Turkey Boy!"
I've got spurs on my feet,
and the chicks all think I'm sweet.
I'm Turkey Boy!

Well, one day I was sitting practising my guitar, when I noticed Red Fred Fox watching me through the fence!

I stopped playing at once.
(You see, Tiny Turk, us turkeys get kind of nervous when foxes are around.)

"Don't stop, Turkey Boy," he said. "You're playin' good!"

"I am?" I said, surprised.

"Sure are," said Red Fred. "But hey, don't just sit there strummin' to thin air, boy. Come and play at the barn dance tonight!"

"Can I?" I gasped.

"You bet your tail feathers!"
said Red Fred.

I was nervous when I stepped on to the stage that night.

My knees were shaking, and my fine, waxy crest trembled with excitement.

But as soon as I started playing,
I felt just fine.

The crowd were great. I played
Turkey Boy, and they went wild.

Then I played my new song, *Black Feather Shake*, and did my special wing-waggle. *Whoo!* The crowd just couldn't get enough!

Red Fred Fox was grinning from ear to ear.

"Turkey Boy!" he told me, "You just got yourself a manager! Stick with me, son, and I'll make you a star!"

Well, that was how it all began.
I played at every barn dance in the
neighbourhood. I was a sensation.

Animals would point at me in the farmyard, and pigeons would fly in from miles around, just to get my autograph.

Red Fred was pleased.
He bought me a new guitar
and my first pair of sunglasses.

Then one day he said,

I nearly fell into the seed tray.

"A *real* record?"
I cried. "Yeah!"

23

So we went uptown to the
recording studio.

We met the owner, a large pig called Colonel Porker.

He had a gold ring in his snout, and he smoked a big, fat cigar.

I played him my song and he grinned.

"Boy," he declared. "When we get that song out on record, you're going to be a STAR!"

And he was right. I had my picture in all the newspapers and magazines. I really was a star!

I stopped travelling around in the back of a farm cart. I got myself a fancy limousine!

I only played the biggest dance halls and the fanciest clubs.

There were posters with my
picture on everywhere.

Everyone said I looked so
handsome.

Wherever I
went, I took one
make-up chick to
polish my fine,
waxy crest…

…and another
to smooth out
my feathers.

32

That's when folks started calling me...the King of the Birds.

Grandpa Turkey sighed and shook his head.

"Then my boy," he continued sadly, "something happened that changed things forever."

It was the night of the big concert.
The biggest gig I had ever played.

I was topping the bill at The
Hollywood Barn!

The hall was packed with animals
and birds all chanting, *"King! King!
King of the Birds!"*

I leapt up on to the stage and
stood in the spotlight. My new silver
cloak dazzled, and the light glinted
off my wonderful, waxy crest.

The crowd loved it. I loved it too.

Then I climbed up on to a big speaker and struck a pose. The crowd went wild.

"Higher! Higher!" they cried.

I climbed even higher.

At the very top I spread my wings dramatically. The crowd went totally crazy.

Then it happened!

I could smell burning. I felt a
sharp pain, and something flopped
over my eyes.

I had climbed too high, and my lovely, waxy crest had melted in the heat from the lights!

I stumbled from the stage and crawled to the dressingroom.

I looked in the mirror. *Oh horror!*
My handsome face was ruined!

My wonderful, waxy crest was
now a horrible dangling mess!

Well, that was the end. It was all over. Red Fred Fox said I should go back to the farm.

"So, that's my story," said Grandpa Turkey. "From rags to riches, and back again. That's why I live on this little farm and not in a big mansion. And that's why my crest looks the way it does…"

"That's really sad, Grandpa,"
said Tiny Turk, shaking his head.
Then a thought struck him.

"Well, it's just that Dad's crest is just like yours, and Uncle Terry's and Uncle Brian's. Did they all have terrible accidents, too?" asked Tiny Turk.

"Er, I must be running along now!" Grandpa Turkey said briskly. "Things to do, people to see… er…um…"

Tiny Turk watched Grandpa Turkey go.

"Grandpa Turkey," he said softly. "Are you sure that tale was *totally* true?"

Look out for these top titles from Orchard Books!

Grandpa Turkey's Tall Tales by Jonathan Allen

❑ King of the Birds   1 84121 877 4   £3.99
❑ And Pigs Might Fly   1 84121 710 7   £3.99

Finger Clicking Reads by Shoo Rayner

❑ Rock-a-doodle-do!   1 84121 465 5   £3.99
❑ Treacle, Treacle, Little Tart   1 84121 469 8   £3.99

The One and Only by Laurence Anholt
Illustrated by Tony Ross

❑ Micky the Muckiest Boy   1 86039 983 5   £3.99
❑ Ruby the Rudest Girl   1 86039 623 2   £3.99
❑ Harold the Hairest Man   1 86039 624 0   £3.99

These books are available from all good bookshops,
or can be ordered direct from the publisher:
Orchard Books, PO BOX 29, Douglas IM99 1BQ
Credit card orders please telephone 01624 836000 or fax 01624 837033
or e-mail: bookshop@enterprise.net for details.

To order please quote title, author and ISBN and your full name and address.
Cheques and postal orders should be
made payable to 'Bookpost plc'.
Postage and packing is FREE within the UK
(overseas customers should add £1.00 per book).

Prices and availability are subject to change.